The Haunting of Excelsior Hotel

Riley Amitrani

The Excelsior: The Grand Opening….

Blackpool UK, circa 1925

The Excelsior was a grand addition to the seaside town of Blackpool in the early 1900's as a luxury accommodation to what had become a popular resort community on the shores of the Irish Sea of England. The construction of the expansive hotel was lauded by everyone as the perfect addition to the attractions that already drew flocks of Brits there, such as the Blackpool Tower and Pleasure Beach. Prior to its completion, there were only modest accommodations available, and the more well-to-do travelers flooded its doors as the elegant touches there spoke to their self-proclaimed status. With the rise of The Excelsior, Blackpool was transformed from an attraction of the common man of industrialized England of the 19th century, to one of a major resort community aimed at the elite as the economy evolved with the advent of the next century.

The increase in Blackpool's population was attributed to the change in the seaside resort's character and no one could deny that the stately Excelsior was not at the epicenter of it all. The locals had a new source of employment and despite what some saw as a possible clash of class lines between the guests of the hotel and the people who were responsible for keeping it running, nothing ever manifested in that regard. Granted there was little if any intermingling among the guests and its employees, but there was as well no overt sign of any trouble between the two groups either. The employees and other businesses in town that relied on The Excelsior for their livelihood realized that situation and never showed any resentment toward those more fortunate than themselves who frequented the hotel.

All was well and prosperous for all those connected to The Excelsior at all levels, and word soon spread about the idyllic atmosphere that was available to all who could afford to stay there. As well, the dip in the economic fortunes of other towns in Britain drew many new residents to Blackpool as there seemed to be unlimited opportunity for work at the Blackpool resort. However, in 1925, though it was not immediately apparent, a curious and macabre cloud was falling over the once stylish hotel. On August 23, a man by the name of Harold Grant checked into The Excelsior and was assigned to room 33. Harold was not well-known as a lot of the guests of the hotel were at the time, but he would certainly not have been out of place among the average type of guest of that day either.

Harold checked in alone and went straight to his room to settle in, asking not to be disturbed as he needed to rest after a long journey from London. He paid in cash up front and pre-paid for several days, stating he was unsure of how long he might want to take the room. No one thought more of it, as Harold was just another of the faceless, wealthy customers the staff dealt with every day. The bellman dropped off the luggage for him as usual, and thanked him profusely for the generous tip…it was not an outrageous gratuity, but just perhaps a bit more than what the bellman was normally accustomed to.

The staff returned to its regular routine as it was shaping up to be a busy weekend, as lots of visitors were arriving to take a last-minute vacation before the warm temperatures of the summer were chased away by the arrival of fall. The bellman and his assistants moved constantly up and down the floors as more and more guests checked in. They passed by room 33 numerous times as the afternoon went on, but at no time did anyone notice anything out of the ordinary about the room other than the "do not disturb" sign hung from the door knob. Perhaps unusual for that time of day, but they never questioned anything one of their guests might do, as long as it was within the decorum of day. Many of their visitors were what were often described generously as "eccentric" and there was not an employee anywhere from top to bottom who could not suffer these eccentricities in lieu of the tip they might lose by saying anything.

A few hours after Harold had checked in, the rush of arrivals began to slow and the host at the registration desk was able to relax. He had just drawn himself a quick cup of tea when he was summoned to the lobby by what was clearly a very distressed guest. It was a major part of his job to keep everyone pleased and carefree in their stay. The last thing he wanted was any sign of commotion or a flap from one of the guests that might spill over and tarnish the stellar reputation of The Excelsior…the owner had made this very clear upon hiring Ted Ingalls. He could see such a situation now brewing just across the way and he abandoned his tea without even a taste to keep the situation from escalating any further.

As he left his station, he was already being summoned with great urgency by the man he had spotted as the man was helping his wife to a chair, her demeanor giving off the impression she might just keel over at any moment. Another part of Ingalls' key responsivities was to have complete recall of all the guests' names, so that a more personal touch could be used for all interaction with their elite clientele. Especially when addressing a problem. This was one of the owner's non-negotiable mandates. And so far, Ted Ingalls had to agree that implementing this strategy was often helpful in calming the frayed nerves of more irate guests, regardless of how minor the issue.

"Mr. Andrews," Ingalls said as he approached the couple, "what has happened?"

"It's our room, man!" the obviously distraught and annoyed Andrews spit at him.

"Your room? Is something not to your satisfaction?"

"Hardly! You can see how it has nearly incapacitated my wife!"

Ingalls looked over at the obese lump of a woman who could barely fit in the oversized chair. He was used to catering to all manner of demands, so he immediately put on his best face of empathy and compassion as he looked with great concern on the woman as her husband frantically fanned her while she moaned as if in great distress.

"I can see, Mr. Andrews! Please tell me the problem and I will take care of it immediately."

"It's the stench, man! Our room smells like some sort of foul cess pit!"

"Cess pit, sir?"

"Yes! It is hard to narrow it down exactly, but the primary problem is it reeks of sulfur!"

"Sulfur! Oh, dear, that will not do. I am very sorry. How about we move you to our

Executive Suite at no extra charge on an upper floor?"

"Yes. Thank you. That would be wonderful."

"Can I do anything else to help? Maybe call a physician to make sure Mrs. Andrews is alright?"

"No, thank you very much. I think she just needs to rest here. Maybe get her some fresh air."

"As you wish, sir. I will have our staff transfer all your belongings to the new suite. Please come see me when it is convenient and I will give you the new key. And again, please accept my deepest apologies for the inconvenience."

The man just waved him away as he returned to attend to his wife. Ingalls strode off to the front desk and made a visibly vocal order to two of his bellman to check it out. It was just loud enough to make sure that the Andrews could hear him, but not so loud as to upset anyone else that might have been within ear shot. It was a skill he had honed over time to appease his overly sensitive guests.

"Thomas! William! Please check out room 32. There is an overpowering odor of sulfur that has made it impossible for the Andrews to stay there any longer. Move all their belongings to the executive suite, number 118, immediately and then go back and find out what is going on up there and get it fixed!"

The bellmen hustled off at once, playing along with their supervisor's drama. This had not been the first time the three of them had performed such theater for a guest and they knew the drill. They all knew it was most probably just some minor smell that had drifted in from the shore. A lot of their guests were not accustomed to the various scents that were common here on the Irish Sea coast…it was a common complaint. Ingalls looked up to see Mr. Andrews helping his whale of a wife through the lobby and outside as she continued to moan and wail. Ingalls smiled at the man as he nodded his approval at the swift action taken.

As soon as the Andrews were out of sight though, Ingalls simply shook his head and stifled a laugh as he went back to his tea and the afternoon paper. He had just taken a brief taste of the brew when both Thomas and William were back at the reception desk, both looking as if they had seen a ghost. They said nothing, but just stood and grasped the edge of the desk.

"Are you two alright? You look as if you've seen a ghoul?"

"No, Mr. Ingalls, not a ghoul." Thomas replied as he was now supporting his companion from falling over.

"Did you move the Andrews' belongings and find out what they were talking about?"

"No, sir." Thomas said weakly as William was beginning to recover a bit.

"No? And why would that be?"

"I think that maybe you had better come see for yourself, sir." Thomas said in a whisper.

Ingalls was about to refuse when he got a good look into Thomas' eyes. This was not a man who rattled easily, but in those eyes, he could see that the man was clearly shaken. He had another man take the desk and he and Thomas returned to room 32 while Harold sat quietly on a chair behind the desk, his head in his hands. As they came down the hall, Ingalls knew immediately that the odor that the Andrews had complained about was no scent wafting off the shore. The closer they got to room 32, the more noticeable the stench got and once in the room, both men immediately covered their mouths and noses.

"My word, man, that is horrible!" Ingalls exclaimed before he ran back to the hallway. "Any idea where it is coming from?"

Thomas just moved backward and pointed at room 33. The mere thought of going back in there was out of the question.

"Mr. Grant's room? You went in already?"

Thomas just nodded and began to tremble. The door to 33 was still slightly ajar and Ingalls pushed it open tentatively with one hand. What had been merely noticeable in room 32 was nearly overpowering in the room where Harold Grant resided. With great effort, Ingalls covered his mouth and nose and walked just inside the room to see the apparently unconscious form of Harold Grant splayed across the bed. Ingalls stumbled back to the hallway to join Thomas, both of them now sitting against the far wall, their knees drawn up high.

"Did you check for a pulse, Thomas?"

"Yes, sir, Nothing. But his face! Did you see it, sir?"

Ingalls just nodded. He unfortunately had. He wished with all his heart that he had not, but it was too late for wishing. The tortured and twisted visage on Grant's face was something Ingalls was sure would haunt him for the rest of his days. Not sure exactly how to handle the situation, Ingalls went to the owner who assured him the man had probably just had a sudden heart attack or some such thing.

"He just went up there and that was it, right, Ingalls?"

"Yes, sir."

"Looked completely exhausted and asked not to be disturbed upon check-in?"

"Yes, sir."

"Then there it is, man. Call the coroner, air out the room and that is that."

"What about the other guests, sir?"

The look from his boss could have turned him to stone. Ingalls knew just to follow his orders and he did as the man had told him. After the coroner had come and gone, the story shared with any curious guests was just that one of the employees had suffered a sudden and fatal heart attack. The last thing to be passed along was that one of their fellow travelers might have fallen ill. *An employee?* That was of no mind. But to suggest another guest had succumbed was, as his boss had suggested many moons ago, "just bad for business".

The maids changed out all of the linens and scoured the room completely. By the time they had finished, whatever had been the source of the nauseating sulfuric odor had vanished...as if it had never been there at all. They all went back to their routines, and no one other than Ingalls, the owner, and the two bellmen knew the true story. The only real fallout from the incident was that both Thomas and William never came back to work at The Excelsior. They did not give notice or even come and talk to Ingalls. They just disappeared.

The owner and staff assumed it was just some sort of inexplicable phenomenon and thought no more of that day. Until, that is, the same exact thing happened with the next three guests that were checked in to room 33. The staff did their best to cover up the pattern of events that had become routine with staying in room 33. Despite knowing it was biting into the bottom line, the owner finally had no other choice but to no longer rent out room 33. They merely posted a renovation sign across the doorway of the room. Their clientele were still in the dark as to what was actually going on there, but the owner knew it would only be a matter of time before they could no longer cover it up and that would likely be the beginning of the end for The Excelsior as word spread.

The years went by and a number of new owners took over The Excelsior. Each time, room 33 was reopened and in each time the same pattern repeated itself. It took mere hours before a resident of room 33 was found stone dead with the same terrifying mask of horror on their faces. Each new owner ignored the stories that were bandied about as they assumed ownership, somehow seeming to have to have it happen to them first-hand before believing it themselves. Even today, in 2016, this pattern has manifested itself. However, the current owner, Anne Cartwright, needed just a single taste of this. Between the old tales of the room and what she had seen, she immediately closed off the room permanently.

She had always been a rational and well-grounded person prior to arriving to run The Excelsior, but she had been so shocked and petrified when it happened to her, she asked no more questions. She was not sure what was going on nor why. She just knew she was not going to let it happen anymore on her watch. No renovation sighs were posted. The room was just no longer made available. Under any circumstances.

The Excelsior: Under New Management…yet again

Blackpool, UK, December 24, 2016

Chloe Riddell had driven most of the day, and if not for the urgency of her trip, she was not sure she could have kept going. She had finished her university program only with the financial support of beloved grandmother, Emily. Chloe's parents had been tragically killed in a freak airline accident while she has in her third year of school while her father had been attending a conference in Spain. Her mother did not normally accompany him in these regular jaunts, but for some reason she had gone along this time. Despite being shattered emotionally over the loss, Chloe was sure that was it for her education.

There had been some money that had come to her from the life insurance policy, but it had not covered her mother at all. That situation, coupled with the funeral expenses, had drained the vast majority of the settlement. It would allow her some meager living expenses, but there was no way it would even come close to paying the remainder of her school bills. She was about to call it quits when her Grandmother Emily stepped in. Emily was what today might have been termed a free spirit, but in her day, she was seen as rebellious…labelled the "black sheep" of the family and shunned. Her father had given up looking for her once he gone away to university himself, based on the lies his relatives fed him.

The family had written her off and he was told, erroneously, that she had died during one of her "wild trips". In fact, Chloe had not seen her grandmother since she was about ten or so, and was crushed when she got the same line that was fed to her father. When this older woman appeared at her parents' funeral she was rocked to her core to be reunited with her once again.

"Is it really, you?" Chloe asked as the woman first took her hands and then hugged her tight at the memorial service.

"It is dear…so sorry I let those bastards of a family we fell in with coerce me away from you."

"Where have you been? What have you been doing?"

"Later, Chloe…this is not the time or place. Let's honor your parents. Then we will talk."

After all the furor of the services were over and all the dust had settled, Chloe and Emily sat and talked all night. Emily explained that she could no longer stay where she had been due to a lot of choices she had made early in life and how judgmental and disapproving all their relatives had been. She had made sure her son had enough money to go to school or pursue whatever it was he might choose in life and then just faded out of the picture.

"I know it may sound cold and heartless now, but they were taking it all out on your father as well. It was best for everyone."

"Even me?"

Emily fell silent and winced.

"I know it was horribly unfair to you as a child, Chloe, but trust me, it would have been much worse otherwise. Those vile people I was unfortunate enough to be related to would have poisoned you against me. I would rather have had you think me dead somewhere that let that happen."

"But you came back now…."

"I did. Chloe…getting old has a few advantages that you will discover when you reach my age. One of those is that you eventually cease caring what others think of you and you no longer feel the need for their approval."

Chloe smiled at her with great admiration.

"And besides. Most of them are dead anyway."

Chloe burst into laughter with her grandmother, realizing it was the first time she had laughed since getting the news of her parents' deaths. As the night went on, Chloe relayed her financial woes. Emily did not frown nor look the least bit upset which Chloe found unsettling to be sure. Emily could see that her granddaughter was baffled by her lack of empathy at her perceived situation and immediately jumped in to put her mind at ease. She never exactly said where or how it was that she had come to have the funds, but Emily assured Chloe that as long as she was able, there was no way that her education was to be cut short.

And so, it was that on one of the worst nights of her life, Chloe was gifted with an endowment that was earmarked for her educational expenses. She graduated with honors and never forgot her grandmother, Emily. They stayed in touch constantly following her matriculation, and Chloe dedicated all her work, mostly privately, and when it was appropriate, publicly, to the woman who had made her successes possible. It was with these memories that Chloe now pushed herself mile after mile to reach the assisted care facility in Blackpool where Emily was now living.

Chloe had been hoping that she and her new boyfriend, Jack Sutter, would be able to spend a few days at the holidays together, but Jack had just started a new job and at the moment it was not possible for him to get away beyond anything more than just Christmas Day. Then, just the day before Christmas Eve, Chloe had gotten an emergency call from the facility where Emily was living, letting her know that her grandmother had taken an unexpected downturn in her health and that it might be a good time to visit. They could not give her an exact time frame based on the imprecise nature of predicting her time left based on the myriad of health problems she had.

As well, and what spurred Chloe out the door, even at the possible threat of losing her own job, was that Emily had been asking for her every day now for the last week. Chloe knew she was probably the only family that her grandmother still had around—certainly the only family that would deem it proper to care about her anymore. And besides…if not for the kindness of her grandmother's heart and spirit, Chloe knew she would most likely be waiting tables or working as a barista in some generic coffee shop back in Southampton. The emergency trip was nothing she wanted to burden Jack with, and at the moment it seemed as if this would work out fine for both of them. She was still crestfallen over missing the holidays with Jack, but seeing as how he only had the one day off, she felt not quite as bad. There would be other holidays together, and where she needed to be right now, totally undistracted by anything, was Blackpool with her grandmother.

Chloe plied herself with caffeine and loud music on the radio and cold air from the open windows as she made the long and emotional journey north toward Blackpool.

She was not familiar at all with Blackpool itself. She knew of it vaguely from having seen it mentioned in travel brochures around town and even a short project she had done for her graphic arts firm for the newly vamped amusement park that sat atop Pleasure Beach. She pulled into Blackpool and made the rounds through town to find lodging for the night. In her haste to get out of Southampton, it had just never crossed her mind that she would be arriving into a popular shoreside resort town on Christmas Eve.

In retrospect, she realized her lack of foresight, but the call from the care facility had overridden all her rational thought processes. All she wanted to do once she could get off from work, was to get on the road and get to her grandmother's bedside. However, after being turned away by six or seven places, the reality of her situation began to settle over her like a shroud. Chloe was about to give up and was seriously considering just sleeping in the car, though she was hardly prepared for a frigid night in her car. As she cruised down the Lytham Street in town, she looked ahead to see a modest-looking hotel, The Excelsior.

She seemed to recall from something she had read somewhere that The Excelsior had fallen from its once lofty standing, but she could not recall the circumstances. The average-looking structure ahead did not inspire her to rush to check it out, but at this point, Chloe thought it might be this place or nothing at all. She parked and climbed the steep steps that led to the unassuming, yet festively decorated entrance. With great hope in her heart, Chloe approached the reservation desk and a woman in her mid-fifties looked up from her writing and smiled as she pushed a lock of graying hair behind her ear.

"Welcome, Miss…I'm Anne Cartwright, the owner. May I help you?"

"I hope so, Ms. Cartwright. Would you by any chance have a room available for the night?"

"No reservation?"

"I am afraid not."

"I'm terribly sorry, Miss. But it's Christmas Eve. We are booked solid."

Chloe felt like the whole world was slipping out from under her feet as she slumped against the desk and her eyes filled with tears. Anne rushed from behind the counter and caught Chloe by the shoulders as it appeared she might fall to the floor.

"Easy, child…come with me."

Anne walked Chloe to the small but cheery lobby where a lively fire was already crackling away. She handed Chloe a glass of water and let gather her emotions. After thanking Anne for the water and her concern, Chloe looked into her face and fighting back fresh tears, explained her situation. No one in town had a room and all she wanted to do was spend Christmas with her grandmother, as her last surviving family member. Anne was deeply moved by the story and could see just how exhausted and desperate the poor girl was. Reluctantly, Anne told Chloe the long history associated with room 33 and why she had vowed never to rent it out again.

Chloe brightened at the prospect of there actually being something available at last. Anne's tale was indeed bizarre and strange, but Chloe was just not the type of person to buy into all that "haunted room" nonsense. After much insistence on her part, Chloe finally got Anne to relent and she checked her into room 33. The room had not been let out in almost twenty-five years. Anne was still unsure as she helped Chloe get her things from the car and into her room, but surely after all this time, whatever had been cursing that room would have long since departed. That is what Anne told herself even as she came back down the hall to the lobby. But even as she stood in front of the roaring fire, not feeling the slightest bit of warmth from the flames, she prayed she had not just made a huge mistake.

Room 33: Ooooh that smell ...can't you smell that smell?

Chloe stood in the middle of the room and just looked around. Anne had on some level given her the shivers with all her stories of people who checked in to the room but never checked out alive. But as far as she could tell it was just another unremarkable hotel room. It was a simple double bed, a pair of elegantly carved oaken bedside tables, a small dresser with drawers, and a small desk and chair just in the corner, next to a window that looked out toward the sea. Chloe lifted her suitcase from the floor and set it gently on the bed. She checked out the tiny bath that was just off the left side of the bed. A dim light illuminated a ceramic tub with a shower and toilet and sink. Nothing fancy, but also nothing to give her any cause for alarm. *Boy...she had really let the owner spook her.*

Chloe shouldered off her winter coat and hung it on the middle hook of a three-hook hanger set into the wall just behind the door. She sat on the bed and took out her cell phone to call Jack to let him know shew had arrived safely and that she had secured a hotel for the night. As the call rang, Chloe just looked around and shook her head as she laughed to herself at all the hoops she had just had to jump through with Anne Cartwright over the supposed curse that room 33 held.

"Chloe! Good to hear from you. All set?" Jack asked.

"I am but it was an ordeal!"

Chloe sat back against the headboard and regaled Jack with how close she had come to possibly having to spend the night in her car as well as the superstition and legend of the one room available at The Excelsior.

"You are kidding, right?" he asked.

"Not at all. I thought the poor woman was going to pass out right in front of me as she told me the long and fantastical stories that have surrounded this room since the hotel was built."

"Think there might be something to it, Chloe?"

"I have no idea. All I know is it is a normal hotel room. A bit boring, but normal. I thought maybe she was trying to gouge me since it is Christmas Eve, but that was no it at all. For whatever reasons, she really seems to believe it all."

"Incredible…."

They talked a few more minutes and then Chloe hung up to unpack and get her bearings on Blackpool so she could see if the home where her grandmother was now living was perhaps within walking distance. The dresser was small, but seeing as how Chloe had only packed for maybe two days at the most, it was fine. It was still digging at her that she could not stay longer, but her boss had made it clear that she needed to be back in the office no later than the 27th of December. Besides spending Christmas

Day with her grandmother, Chloe also needed to have a conversation with whoever was in charge there to get a more accurate picture of her grandmother's condition and see if anyone could give her a better idea of just how long she might have left.

As he closed the top drawer of the dresser and went to the bathroom to set out her toiletries, Chloe began to detect the unmistakable odor of what smelled like rotten eggs. It was faint at first, but the longer she focused on it, the stronger it seemed to be getting. She went back to the main room and sniffed around trying to see if she could locate the source of the rapidly strengthening stench. No matter where she went in the room, there seemed to be no real origin of the smell. Even a thorough search in the bathroom did not seem to be indicating where it was coming from. It was like in was coming from everywhere all at once.

Considering that it might simply be some rotted scent carrying over from the shore,

Chloe popped open her window to check. Nothing. In fact, the air outside that was drifting in from the mild breeze coming off the sea was clean and fresh. She left the window open for a bit in hopes of airing out her room. Maybe, she thought, it was just some leftover foulness since, according to Anne, the room had not been let out in over twenty-five years. However, even after trying this, when Chloe closed the window again, the odor was just as obvious, if not even more so. Running the water in the sink and the shower did not alleviate the smell either. Covering her mouth and nose, Chloe fled the room to let Anne know and see what could be done to fix it.

As Chloe breathed in deeply of the fresh air in the hallway and made her way back to the reception desk and the lobby, she had a feeling that this was why the room was not being let out. It was not the curse that Anne had so dramatically explained, but simply the persistent stench there was making the room uninhabitable. Chloe supposed it was easier to scare people off with a story of unexplained deaths there than knowing they could not have guests think there was some sort of chemical leak somewhere. If that got out, she reasoned, it would not be long before no one would want to patronize the place at all. From all appearances, The Excelsior looked to be just hanging on as it was. Historically, it had certainly seen better days.

The reception desk was unattended when Chloe arrived, and she finally spotted Anne sunk into a chair near the fireplace, a tumbler of some dark liquor in her hand. She was staring blankly into the flames, almost as if she were staring through them rather than at them as Chloe arrived at her side. Chloe did not want to startle the woman, as she had apparently not heard her approach, so she reached out and touched Anne gently on the arm to get her attention. The woman flinched smartly at her touch and gasped, sloshing a bit of her drink onto the floor.

"I'm sorry, Ms. Cartwright. I did not mean to sneak up on you."

"Oh, no worries, dear. Was just lost in my thoughts, I guess."

However, despite her reply, Chloe could see that the woman had something on her mind other than 'her thoughts'. She looked about as worried and concerned as anyone could be on Christmas Eve.

"Anything wrong?" Anne asked.

Chloe thought that an odd initial response, but if the noxious smell in her room was a known entity, then perhaps not.

"Just my room." Chloe replied.

A visible shiver passed through Anne's frame as soon as those words were out of Chloe's mouth. As well, Chloe could not help but sense that Anne was shocked to even be seeing her. Whatever might be the truth surrounding room 33, apparently Anne had bought into the story she had told earlier. Chloe suppose if that was the case, then according to the superstition, she should already be dead. Prone on her bed with a twisted grimace of horror, pain and revulsion on her face.

"Did you see something?" Anne asked as her hand holding the glass with the remaining liquor began to tremble. It was impossible to miss that this was most likely not her first drink of the evening.

Again, Chloe was utterly puzzled by her reaction.

"No, it's not that, ma'am. It's the smell."

What little color that was remaining in Anne's face quickly drained away as she clasped the tumbler with both hands and looked away from Chloe and back at the fire.

"Ma'am? Ms. Cartwright?" Chloe asked wondering if the woman was actually right in the head.

"Sorry, dear...a smell you say?" She struggled in her reply, her words slurred, partly from the alcohol and partly from what looked to Chloe as sheer fear.

"Yes. Like rotten eggs. It's everywhere. I cannot figure out where it is coming from. Maybe there is a plumbing problem since it has been empty for so long? I was hoping maybe someone here could drop by and take a look?"

"Come into the room? Oh, no…that would not be possible."

"Excuse me? Everyone off for the holidays already?"

"It's not that, dear. It's just…well…"

"Let me guess." Chloe said cutting her off abruptly. "The curse?"

"Actually…yes. Ever since the last episode there, no one here goes in there." Anne tried to offer a weak smile but it just came off as forced.

"You have got to be kidding me. Is this how you treat guests here?" Chloe was trying to keep her temper, but dealing with this preposterous legend was beginning to annoy her.

"No, dear. It's just that room. I told you about the smell and what happens there. It almost always smells like that. Especially just before…" her voice trailed off as she took a healthy slug from her drink.

Chloe had had enough. She knew she came from a larger, more sophisticated background that what was likely in Blackpool, but this was too much. Her temper often got her in trouble routinely, so Chloe reluctantly took the advice her grandmother had given her as a young child:

"Do not let your emotions control you, Chloe. When you get mad, take a breath, count to ten, and relax."

Chloe exhaled calmly once she had reached ten and magically the knee jerk reaction to lash out at the hotel owner was gone.

"OK. Fine. Then can a get some bleach so I can flush the pipes?" Chloe asked.

Anne nodded and led her to a closet just off the reservation desk and handed her the bleach. She watched as Chloe went back down the hall and disappeared into her room. Anne refilled her glass with the bourbon that she was slowly drowning herself in ever since leaving Chloe at her room earlier. Her eyes filled with tears as she plodded, unsteadily back to her chair in the lobby and the fire.

Room 33: You Have <u>Got</u> to be Kidding Me…

Despite having heeded her grandmother's advice and having remained calm in Anne's presence, Chloe found herself putting a death grip on the two bottles of bleach as she stomped back down the hall, rolling her eyes at the staff of The Excelsior. It was unbelievable to her that a hotel, in this day and age, was allowing fables and ghost stories to be more of a driving factor in how they ran their business than in reality and good customer service. The smell was just as overpowering as she returned to the room and she hurried to the bath to douse all the accessible plumbing with a healthy dose of bleach. As she emptied one bottle, she was now not sure what was worse, the original sulfur-like smell or the current mixture of sulfur overlaid with the strong chlorine odor.

What she did know was that she could not tolerate either and that maybe it would be a good idea to just let the bleach settle into the pipes and do its thing. She had not eaten since leaving Southampton, and this seemed like a good time to both grab a quick bite of supper while the plumbing got treated. Besides, if she was going to eat, it might be a good idea to go now before it got too late and everyone was closed up in observance of Christmas Eve. She grabbed her coat and keys and closed the door behind her as she headed to the lobby and then out.

Chloe was about to ask Anne for some recommendations for a good place to go to eat, when she glanced into the lobby and saw a glass tumbler, empty, on the floor beside the chair where she had first found Anne. The woman was hidden by the high back of the chair, but Chloe could see her arm hanging over the arm rest, her pale fingers just above the drained glass. Concerned that something bad had occurred, Chloe rushed to the chair to check on the hotel owner. She was immediately relieved that she was fine…still breathing and all…just passed out she guessed.

Chloe set the crystal tumbler on the short table that was in the center of the lobby between the fireplace and the chair, now holding the unconscious Anne Cartwright. Her face looked a bit disturbed as she breathed easily in and out, but otherwise seemed as if she had just overdone it. The nearly three-quarter empty bourbon bottle on the table seemed to confirm that assessment. *Great*, Chloe said to herself…*in addition to a staff scared of their own shadows, they've got a drunk running the joint.* She straightened Anne in the chair, putting her arm that had been flailing over the arm rest in her lap before covering her with an afghan from the nearby sofa.

She guessed anyone coming in was on their own, though Anne had indicated that they were full anyway. Chloe snugged her coat up to her chin and took one last look at the snoozing Anne Cartwright. She guessed she had done all she could for the moment…and much like everyone else here at The Excelsior, she saw was on her own as she walked out to find an open café. The sun was just heading for the horizon as Chloe set off down the street in search of some food. Clouds were beginning to gather as well, and the once crystal-clear sky was now well overcast and the threat of snow looked quite likely as the calm breezes that had been blowing off the sea had intensified as well.

Despite the small town, it seemed as if Chloe would have her pick of at least a few cafes and restaurants along the few streets of the town within close walking distance of The Excelsior. She was sure had she waited just a little longer that she would have been shut out as merchants would be shutting up soon to head home to be with their families. After walking for longer than she had anticipated, especially in the wind, Chloe spotted a brightly-lit pub, The Albert and the Lion, just ahead on her left. After all the weirdness at the hotel, Chloe thought a lively pub might be just the ticket to get her mind off room 33. She leaned into the wind and jogged across the street and into the pub.

The Albert and the Lion seemed to be quite popular, even on this day, and the warmth of the interior, the clinking of glasses, and the upbeat conversation among the patrons as she stepped toward the bar made Chloe smile. In addition to the situation back at The Excelsior, Chloe was feeling more and more alone with Jack back in Southampton. She slipped off her hood and pushed her hair back as a waitress made her way to greet her.

"Welcome to The Albert and the Lion, miss. First time here?"

"It is. Just in town for the holidays."

"Just yourself, then?"

"Afraid so." Chloe replied, feeling just a bit depressed.

"Not to worry, miss…" the waitress replied, sensing her mood. "We'll make you feel right at home. This booth OK?"

Chloe nodded and slid in after hanging her coat on the hook at the booth.

"Something to drink?" the waitress asked.

"Pint of your best, please."

She looked around, and although she was a stranger, she noticed several of the other customers raising their glasses her way and wishing her a Merry Christmas. She still felt a bit isolated, but in an odd way, the simple gestures from the locals warmed her heart as he raised her pint in return. Chloe was still trying to prepare herself for the trip to the convalescent home and her grandmother as well as doing her best to forget room 33. The warm reception here, without having to ward off any unwanted advances from the male customers was making all of that easier to process in her brain.

She ordered what looked like a decadent cheeseburger platter to go with her beer as she removed the small paperback from her purse to read as she ate. As time went on, the crowd inside began to thin out, surely, Chloe thought, to head home for family obligations. The burger was even better than it had looked in the menu and she was well into her second pint before she looked up to see that she was just one of a couple patrons remaining. Embarrassed that she had gotten so caught in her book, she suddenly wanted to be anywhere else, afraid that she might be causing the staff to stay late on her account. Her waitress saw her plight and came immediately to ease her mind.

"I'm so sorry, miss...I just lost track of time. I am sure you need to close up and get home."

"No need to worry. My husband and I own the place. That's him, the big hairy bloke at the bar."

Chloe looked over and he tipped two fingers at her in a mock salute and smiled broadly.

"We live just upstairs and this is more home to us anyway. You take your time. Seems like you maybe have something on your mind that is not so holly jolly, if you will excuse my asking."

Chloe closed her book as the waitress sat across from her in the booth. It must have been written all over her face. Jack had been right. Chloe would have made a lousy poker player. She wiped away at tear and sighed.

"I…uh….shit…." Chloe started. "No need to burden you at the holidays, miss."

"Nonsense. And it's Linda. Linda Moore."

"I'm Chloe. Chloe Riddell." They shook hands and Chloe spilled her guts. First about her grandmother in the home nearby and that this might be her last holiday with her, and then being away from Jack on their first Christmas together as a couple.

Linda offered Chloe a tissue and listened compassionately as the story unfolded.

"Sorry to hear all that, Chloe, but glad we could make it all go away for a few hours anyway. You have relatives you are staying with in Blackpool?"

"No. Just here to visit my grandmother. Seems she and I are the last of the line. Was able to get just a couple days off from my job in Southampton to come see her, then back home. Got a room for the next night or two here in town. The Excelsior."

As soon as the words were off her lips, she noticed a subtle but definite change in Linda's demeanor, though the kind waitress/owner tried to cover.

"Did you say The Excelsior?" Linda asked quietly, as if she might be overheard, despite them being virtually thon only ones left in the pub at the moment.

"Yeah. It was slim pickings to get a room when I got here, but they had one room left, lucky for me. You seem like you are familiar with it. I hear it used to be quite a grand place."

"Um…in its day, it was. Back when it was first built."

"So, what happened?"

"Oh, you know, it went through lots of owners, then the economic dips we all had to suffer through. I guess the grandeur just became a bit beyond most people's wallets."

"Sure…sure."

"Chloe? Can I ask you something?"

"Shoot…"

"You said you looked all over town and finally got the last room available at The Excelsior?"

"Yep."

"Are you familiar with the stories there?"

"You mean the people checking in and then being dead a few hours later. Looks of horror on their faces? Those stories?" Chloe smirked as she replied.

"So, you <u>have</u> heard." Linda was no longer smiling.

"Yeah, yeah…I don't really buy into all of that, no offense."

"None taken. But they did not actually book you into room 33, did they?"

"As a matter of fact, they did. It was all that was open. Christmas Eve and all, you know."

Linda then physically sat back from her as if she was afraid something from the woman from Southampton might rub off on her.

"When did you check in?"

"Oh…maybe three, four hours ago, I guess, why?"

"Just curious. I know we just met, but could I offer some friendly advice?"

"Sure…"

"Go back there, get your things and get out."

"Are you serious, Linda?"

"Deadly." she said, at once regretting her choice of words as she winced.

"Oh, come on, Linda…surely you do not believe all this whoey?"

Linda just looked her straight in the eyes and said nothing.

"OK…just for the sake of argument. Suppose it is all true. How come I have been there all this time so far and I am still up and walking around?"

"No idea. Maybe because no one has been in the room for so long. Who knows. You smelling like rotten eggs in the room yet?"

"Actually, yeah…that is why I am here. I doused the plumbing with some bleach and wanted to give it time to clean out the smell before I flush the chlorine funk out."

"I am begging you, Chloe. Do not stay there tonight. Or any other night."

"Blackpool's full up. Where exactly am I supposed to go?"

"Come stay with me and my husband. We've got plenty of room."

"I appreciate your concern, Linda. Really, I do. But this is just crazy! I'll be fine. Go help your husband close up and have a great Christmas. I'll be here for at least another day or so. I'll come by to say goodbye, just so you can see all of these stories are just that…stories and nothing more."

"Please, Chloe…"

Chloe just stood and hugged Linda and headed back to the hotel after paying them. Linda stood at the door of The Albert and the Lion as her husband put his arm around her waist while they watched Chloe fight her way back down the street, the snow that had looked so promising now flying sideways in the wind.

"You tried, Linda…." her husband said as he pulled her close.

When Chloe went back through the lobby, she saw that Anne had apparently sobered up enough to head off to bed, as all the chairs in the lobby around the fireplace were empty. The fire was still burning, now just reduced to low embers, but the afghan was back in its spot on the sofa and the glass and the nearly empty bourbon bottle gone. Chloe felt better knowing Anne had just tottered off to bed and she continued down the hallway to her room to see what was what. As soon as she opened the door, Chloe was relieved. The room stank of chlorine, but the rotten egg odor was gone.

"Voila!" Chloe said out loud as she tossed her keys on the top of the dresser and hung her coat.

Sure, the smell of chlorine was not ideal, but she knew that all it would take to rid herself of that would be to flush the sink and shower with some hot water for a few minutes. She headed into the bathroom, flushed the toilet a few times and then turned on the hot water to clear out the bleach. While this was going on, Chloe changed for bed and flipped through the TV channels to see if she could find a nice, relaxing Christmas movie to distract her from all the talk of room 33 that seemed to be all over Blackpool. As she slipped her favorite T-shirt over her head, she found "It's a Wonderful Life" playing. The classic she assumed was most likely on a repeating loop as it was most Christmas Eves since she had been a little girl. Sappy, but a classic...just what she needed.

As George Bailey was discovering that he could not serve in the military due to the ear injury he has sustained as a kid, and was to have to do his bit right there in Bedford Falls, Chloe went to the bathroom. She sniffed deeply. All clear. She turned off the water and snuggled down under the thick comforter to watch the movie. Even though Chloe had seen the film maybe a hundred times, she was soon sucked right back into it, wishing evil thoughts on the black-hearted Henry Potter. However, after just a few minutes, Chloe heard this odd humming sound coming from the bathroom. It seemed to be part hum, part vibration, but she could just not figure it out.

She threw off the covers when a commercial break came on to put an end to the annoying buzz. Once there, she saw that the overhead fan was running, assuming she had simply forgotten to turn it off when she was "de-funking" the bathroom. She flipped off the switch. However, as soon as she deactivated the fan, she noticed that the smell of sulfur was back. It was not as intense as before, but there was no mistaking that it had returned. Frustrated, but grateful in the back of her mind that she even had a room for the night, she dumped the second bottle of bleach down all the drains again.

Chloe padded back and jumped into the bed just in time to see that George was beginning to get a taste of what Bedford Falls might have been like if he had never been born. She had no more than taken a good deep breath and settled down again when she heard water running from the bath. In what was becoming a seemingly unending set of annoyances, Chloe angrily threw back the comforter and flipped on the bathroom light to see that the shower was now running. She did not remember putting it on, but there was no other explanation. Chloe cranked off the water to the shower, turning each knob as far off as she could manage. Tired from the travel and stress of her grandmother's situation and all the weirdness of room 33, Chloe slammed the bathroom door and went back to bed deciding not to deal with any of it until morning.

Room 33: What Was It That Everyone Was Saying About This Place Again?

Chloe tried to get back to enjoying the wrap up of "It's a Wonderful Life", but she was so annoyed with the whole day that she found herself getting irritated even with the Frank Capra classic. How she could be getting pissed at this wonderful film was beyond her, so she went back once again to the words of wisdom from her grandmother. She closed her eyes, took some deep relaxing breaths, counted silently to ten and then exhaled slowly. Her Grandmother Emily was a wise woman, but for Chloe this time it was not working…a first time ever for her that it had failed.

The harder she tried, the more aggravated she got. Chloe got up to get some water and the room spun slightly as her stomach pitched. She grasped the bed post to steady herself and closed her eyes once more until the sensation of dizziness passed. Her stomach was still unsettled as she sat on the edge of the mattress, but it was nothing serious. She felt her forehead to see if she might be feverish, praying she was not coming down with a bug of some ilk. Her skin was cool and dry to the touch. *Maybe she had gotten food poisoning from the pub?* It seemed unlikely, but there was always that chance.

She supposed it could have been the beer as well, but a couple of pints of ale, with a full meal, was hardly something to even consider. Chloe knew her tolerance for alcohol, and this was not even in the ballpark. There was always everything else that was going on: a long trip from Southampton in which she had pushed herself with stops along the way only for petrol or bathroom breaks; the stress over her grandmother and what she might find when she arrived at the home; being far away from Jack during the holidays. And then the biggie on top of it all, the stress of nearly not securing a hotel room for the night, finally landing in the one room in all of

Blackpool that everyone there saw as cursed since the day The Excelsior had opened in the 1920's.

Then dealing with Anne Cartwright who was running a hotel where if you wanted something taken care of, it seemed it was up to you. All the tales that were attached to her room would have been easy enough to shrug off if she had not had that conversation with Linda at The Albert and the Lion. She could understand, even if he did not buy into it, older people in Blackpool hanging onto such superstitions, but Linda was about her age. And she was so grounded and rational in everything else that they had talked about. That had really thrown her off. Then again, maybe it was just all the noxious fumes she had probably sucked up since she had checked in: first the rotten egg stench and then the chlorine from the bleach.

As Chloe considered all of this, she decided that it would have be remarkable if she was not coming down with some illness if you looked at all that had gone on for her in the last day or so. It was just cumulative stress from it all, she said to herself. She took a couple aspirin to alleviate the headache that had suddenly arisen and decided that the best remedy to head off anything more serious would be to turn in early and get a good night's sleep. The last thing she needed now was to come down with an illness that would ruin the main purpose of her trip, that of being with her Grandmother Emily.

As she swallowed the aspirin, Chloe felt more centered. Her head was still pounding, but her brief bout of vertigo had passed and the nausea was beginning to fade as well. The movie, now long over, had progressed to some despicable infomercial that was making Chloe spiritually nauseous.

"Really?" she said as she looked at the screen with disdain, *"on Christmas Eve of all times?"*

She clicked off the set and went back to bed. She sniffed deeply as she turned out the light by her bed, but all she smelled was the clean air associated with the shore…with maybe just a faint trace of bleach. It seemed after all, that whatever the source of the sulfur odor, it was confined to the bathroom. Just old plumbing, Chloe thought to herself as she closed her eyes and relaxed. The gentle sound of the waves against the beach filled her ears, and before she knew it she was fast asleep. Chloe was not sure how long she had been asleep, but when she awoke it was still dark outside. She had failed to pack her travel clock and her watch was across the room on the dresser with her keys.

She was feeling OK, just tired, but was confused at why she had even woken up in the first place. The temperature of the room was fine…it was quiet in the hotel as far as she could tell…she did not need to use the bathroom…even her headache and nausea were gone. *So, what was it?* Then, just as she was sinking back into the covers, she knew what it was. The sound was not loud nor readily identifiable, but as she cocked her ear it was impossible to miss. In her semi-conscious state, Chloe initially thought it was her imagination or perhaps a dream remnant, but when the noise kept up, she knew she was wide awake and was not imagining it.

From the other side of the closed bathroom door, a subtle but regular scratching sound was audible. Chloe sat up, still somewhere between groggy and fully awake as she listened more closely. In just a few seconds, the noise repeated itself. It was hard to say exactly what the scritching sound was. Chloe had been around enough animals as a child that she was accustomed to the well-known sound of pets' nails on a door to be let in and what she was hearing was not lining up with that. On the other hand, though she had no experience with what it might sound like for a set of human cuticles to be scraping away, this did not seem exactly right either.

The longer she sat and focused on the disturbance coming from behind the bathroom door, the more her imagination raced and soon her pulse was pounding in her ears and her respirations were coning more rapidly, bordering on gasping as her ragged breaths were getting out of control. Chloe tried to make herself calm down, but it was no use. The harder she tried, the more regular and insistent the scratching sounds seemed to grow. There was not a vocalization associated with the clawing, neither human nor animal, and Chloe was hard pressed to decide if that was helping.

The smell of sulfur was again leaking from around the crevices of the door that was firmly closed as the nails or claws or whatever it was became nonstop, now rattling the door back and forth in its frame. Chloe was sure this must be a dream. It was all that talk of the curse and then how she had let Linda's pleas with her get inside her head. *That was all.* However, when Chloe performed the old wives' tale of pinching herself to test for a dream, the pain was all too real. The noise went on and on and Chloe was feeling herself slipping deeper and deeper into a self-imposed terror that she was afraid would not release her. *What if all that she had been told was not just a superstition after all?* She had, she thought, maybe rolled her eyes one too many times at everyone in Blackpool who had tried their best to warn her off. Try as she might to let her rational mind take over and find a sensible and reasonable explanation for this, she could not.

Room 33: Wonder if Linda and Her Husband's Offer Still Stands?

Chloe clapped her hands to her ears and worked hard, just through sheer will power and wishing, to make the impending assault just go away. Slowly, over the next few minutes, the sounds faded in volume and then just ceased. As if they had never happened at all. As silence fell over her, Chloe let her hands drop to her lap as she looked about the room frantically. She was trying not to, but also would not have been horribly shocked, if whatever had plagued this room for so long might be face-to-face with her at last. The room seemed to be carrying just a tinge of the stench, relative to before, but overall, all else was quiet and just the normal-looking room she had found when she had checked in.

Chloe's hair was plastered to her head with perspiration as large, fat droplets traced down her back and her sides from her arm pits, adding to the chill that has set in when the scratching noises had peaked. She shivered as she sat in her damp bedding, grateful that she was still alone. The slight smell that filled the air was a minor thing, Chloe thought, as she sat on the edge of the mattress and took deep breaths as her heart fell back into a normal rhythm.

"Just a dream…." Chloe said out loud, more, she supposed to convince herself more than anything. *"Just a wicked, bad nightmare."*

She toweled off a bit and changed clothes, dumping her damp T-shirt and pajama bottoms on the floor, and then slipped on a fresh, dry pair of exercise sweats. What she needed, Chloe told herself, was just some fresh air. It would clear her head from the dream and maybe a quick walk would give her the rational explanation for where this had come from and why it had seemed so real. Chloe slipped on her winter boots and her coat from the hook on the wall and went to pick up her keys and a small flashlight from her purse.

However, just as her hand touched the keys, the scratching at the bathroom door once again commenced, this time sounding as if whatever it was that was in there wanted out badly. Chloe whipped her head, in an automatic response, toward the door and realized she had never felt so utterly terrified in all her life. All thoughts of a rational explanation were long gone from her brain, and all she could think of was to take Linda's advice and just get the hell out of this place. Chloe reached for the door that led from her room to the hallway, but the knob seemed frozen in place and the door itself stuck firmly in its frame.

Chloe tugged wildly with all her might, but no matter how hard she pulled and tugged on it, it was no use. In fact, the more struggled with the door, the louder the scratching from the bathroom became. Simultaneously, the smell of sulfur flooded her nose, now at a level that made the earlier levels seem relatively undetectable. Chloe found herself in a near hysterical panic, as if she was on edge of losing her mind as she stumbled away from the door and groped for the telephone to call for help.

All memories of how useless Anne and her staff had been earlier were no longer a concern as Chloe was desperate. As she lifted the receiver to her ear, though, it was dead. Not even a dial tone. In a combination of anger and fright, Chloe flung the receiver aside and raked her hands across the top of the dresser until her shaking hands found her cell phone. The smell was making her gag, and she was fighting off the nausea that was threatening to make her vomit as the scratching at the bathroom door was now more of pounding sound interspersed with what had to be non-human nails or claws. She activated her cell phone. Or at least tried to. When she looked down at the display, she saw that the battery was dead.

In her hysteria, Chloe began to scream in frustration, knowing in the back of her mind that the phone had been fully charged when she had gone to bed. As the stink of the sulfur and the clatter at the bathroom door continued to get stronger, Chloe dumped her purse onto the floor and pawed desperately at the spilled contents until she found the charger for her phone. She plugged in the adapter and then connected her phone, but it was still as dead and useless as it had been before. Chloe threw the phone across the room as she sunk to her knees, buried her face in her hands, and sobbed uncontrollably. Her level of terror and fright was nearly overwhelming her now, and Chloe felt herself slipping metaphorically off a precipice and into madness as she felt utterly lost and at the whims of this God-forsaken room.

When she was sure she could withstand no more, the rancor from the bathroom once again fell suddenly silent, much like a switch had been abruptly thrown. The smell, as well, seemed to be dissipating, and Chloe pushed herself into a sitting position, her back against the dresser. She tried to stand, but her legs would not cooperate. They did not seem to be physically impaired, they simply did not want to support her when she tried to get them under her. She kicked off her boots and crawled back to the bed, pulling herself back onto the mattress and flinging her rubbery legs behind her. With no more energy or strength left, Chloe sunk back under the covers, still clad in all her sweats, as she threw the comforter over her head and closed her eyes tightly.

Despite being back in what seemed like a safe refuge, Chloe could not stop crying and pleading for someone to come help her. She no longer was looking to explain room 33. She just wished she had never checked in in the first place. Or had at least had the good sense to listen to Linda when she had been at The Albert and the Lion. Now, it seemed to Chloe, the four walls of the ordinary-looking hotel room at The Excelsior had become a prison from which she could not escape. Chloe curled into a ball and continued to sob quietly until she fell asleep, her body feeling as if she had just gone a few rounds with an unseen assailant.

She was not sure how long she had been out, but Chloe assume it was just a few minutes as her face was still wet from her tears and sweat as she felt the comforter moving, as if of its own accord. It moved from her head and neck and slid slowly toward the end of the bed. After all that had happened in the last few hours, Chloe kept her eyes clamped tightly shut, petrified at what might now be happening. When she could no longer stand the tension, she opened her eyes just a slit and there at the foot of her bed was the vague outline of person, her comforter bunched in what she assumed were hands.

It was hard for her to know exactly, as the gray light of the room afforded only a rough outline of the figure. It appeared to be a man and was just of average stature, and slightly hunched over as he stood unmoving at her feet. Chloe dared to open her eyes just a bit more, sure that whatever ominous and menacing presence that had been attempting valiantly to escape from the bathroom was now out and waiting for her. As she looked closer, what she saw next made her shake with utter terror and fright. The figure straightened and dropped the handfuls of comforter as the moon just outside her window illuminated his face. Or at least where his face should have been. From the top of the man's head to his throat was just…well…nothing. There were no facial features whatsoever, just smooth, blank skin.

Chloe tried to scream or at least call out as her body shook with uncontrollable tremors. She opened her mouth and tried, but nothing came out. The man never moved from his spot at the foot rest of the bed, but just held his ground and opened his arms as if he was waiting for an embrace from an unseen partner. Convinced that she had completely lost her mind as well as any tentative grasp on whatever bit of reality that was still available to her, Chloe fell back, her mouth opening and closing, almost robotically, as she struggled to cry out, her eyes wide in horror and revulsion.

Meanwhile in Southampton: Have Yourself a Merry Little Christmas, Jack

Jack Sutter arose on Christmas morning, his lone day off from his new job, bored and lonely, missing Chloe more than he had imagined he would. He had known Chloe for a few years, but it was only in the last few months that they had progressed beyond the point of being more than just friends. Jack had never ever imagined that the beautiful Chloe Riddell would ever see him as more than just one of their group of friends that got together regularly for drinks, the occasional film or a concert. He was still amazed when she had confessed that she had felt the same about him. They had laughed long into the night when they both reveled this to one another when Jack had finally worked up his courage to ask her out. They had been virtually inseparable ever since.

He had done his best to support her when the bad news came through about her grandmother. Jack had been adopted and as far as he knew his biological parents as well as any other relatives were no longer around. He had little experience with the bond that Chloe had with Emily, but he did what seemed to him like the right thing as she prepared for her trip to Blackpool. He had even offered to find some way to get some time off from his new job to come along, but in the end, it was impossible. Jack had been out of work for a long time, and after finally securing the job of a lifetime, Chloe would not even consider having him jeopardize it.

Jack, like Chloe, had been crushed when he realized they would be apart for their first Christmas together as a couple, but this just seemed to be how it was to work out this year. Chloe had assured him it would be depressing enough on some level just for her. There was no need to drag him down into the situation as well. They could celebrate when she got back. Maybe combine Christmas with New Year's, she suggested. Jack thought back to that conversation as he stared out his window at the frigid landscape of the neighborhood where he lived. The streets and bare trees were crisp with frost, but so far, no snow had fallen in Southampton, making this a very, very brown Christmas.

He was feeling bad enough, but looking at the bleak scene outside was sure not helping any. Jack brewed himself a strong cup of coffee from the special blend of beans that he and Chloe had discovered during a recent trip to London. He walked to the sofa and sat heavily as the aroma from the fresh coffee filled his nostrils. His first sip of the brew helped, but Jack was undecidedly feeling sorry for himself as his cat, Mortimer, joined him on the couch and curled into a ball at his side.

"Nothing personal, Mort, old man, but this sucks...." Jack said to his roommate.

The cat looked up at him sleepily as he licked his belly. Ah, the life of a cat, Jack mused as he smiled wanly and sipped his coffee. The day was not looking as if the sun was going to make a major appearance and the clouds, while pervasive and solid, did not give off any indication of snow. As Jack finished his coffee, Mortimer moved off to the end of the sofa to snuggle into his favorite blanket. He set the mug aside and glanced over to his laptop that was sitting on the table near the kitchen where Jack had set up a very informal office for himself so he could bring work home if necessary. He was keen to make an impression at the new place and wanted to be prepared to do what he could to make his mark there.

Jack thought back to his conversation with Chloe from last night, and for no reason that he could see at the moment, he went to the desk to see what he could find out about Blackpool and the historic old hotel, The Excelsior. He supposed the wild and bizarre story that Chloe had told him about the old place and the "cursed" room 33 might have spurned it. Besides, he thought, what else am I going to do but sit here and make myself more miserable until Chloe gets back. When Jack was just a kid, he remembered reading something about all the various attractions in Blackpool as a beach retreat, but until Chloe had mentioned The Excelsior, he had never heard of it.

He opened up his browser and began to do a search on the old hotel. There was no shortage of articles on The Excelsior, referencing its origins from the 1920's. Jack was amazed that Chloe had landed a room in such an elaborate and fancy hotel, until he began to come across all the writers who had done all manner of exposes on the old place making it clear that the former showcase hotel for the wealthy was a mere shadow of itself today. The one thing that kept showing up in all the pieces, though, that really caught Jack's attention was the repeated reference to room 33 and its somewhat less than pleasant history.

As Jack read over the articles, he thought back to the stories that Chloe had told him during their call the night before. Like her, Jack was finding himself highly amused at the tales of some sort of "curse" that all the writers had attached to the room. All the accounts, with slight variation, however, aligned very closely with what Chloe had said. Certainly, the locals in Blackpool all seemed to be accepting the superstitions and tall tales without question or doubt, but Jack found the whole thing to be utterly absurd. Perhaps, he mused as he read along, this was another of those tactics used for creating interest and tourist traffic to Blackpool. Jack knew as well as anyone how this strategy had been utilized ad nauseum in Britain as a travel marketing ploy.

The extensive history in England, and elsewhere in Europe, he supposed, was more than adequate to provide such fables and folkloric scenarios to which the gullible traveler might fall prey. The most famous incident that came to his mind at the moment was how the Stanley Hotel in

America had gained a similar notoriety following the publication of Stephen King's "The Shining". That was not to say, Jack thought, that there could possibly be some validity to what might or might not be going on in the historic hotel that sat high in the mountains in Colorado. That was not the point. What might be a commonality, though, between that and room 33 at The Excelsior, was the use of such superstition to take advantage of a gullible public.

Jack was just about to close out his google search engine, when he glanced over at an article, that while it had similar accounts, was focused on a different angle. Oddly enough, the piece had been written just a year earlier. The lone story on the hotel after a long hiatus of interest in the place. The name of the author poked at some recess of Jack's brain, but he could not place it until he began to read through the article more closely. David Woser...of course, now he remembered! Woser had done this lecture when Jack had still been a university student that he had attended with a former girlfriend. The girl had been deep into paranormal research and Jack had tagged along out of sheer curiosity and to humor her. Then, as now, Jack found the whole field laughable, but at the time, as he recalled, his mere agreement to go along had gotten him into the girl's bed that night. Not his proudest moment for sure, but a memorable night nevertheless.

Jack came away from the lecture still as skeptical and dismissive of paranormal activity as he had been before, but what he did remember was that Woser had offered the most scientific and authentic-appearing presentation on the subject he had ever heard. And now, here was Woser again with an investigation into room 33 at The Excelsior. Well…at least he had tried. The article went on in some detail summarizing what all the other half-baked writers had put forth, but in this case, Woser had dug deeper. From interviews and his long history of similar incidents, Woser was suggesting, quite emphatically, that room 33 was the home to a very sinister and demonic presence.

Despite his reputation and respect, at least among the populace that actually bought into this stuff, Woser had been denied access to the room for a thorough investigation. In the article, Woser told of repeated attempts to set up a study in room 33, but the current owner, an Anne Cartwright, was firm in her resolve to keep the room isolated from anyone not associated with the hotel. Much as Chloe had said, Cartwright had sealed off the room from the general public long ago…it had remained locked and unseen by anyone for over twenty years, Woser wrote. *So why, Jack asked himself, did Cartwright finally agree to offer the room to Chloe?*

Woser's article pointed out that the hotel, having fallen on hard times in recent years, was struggling financially, especially during the off-season when people did not think of coming to the shore in Blackpool. However, despite that hardship, Cartwright was adamant about not making room 33 available. Jack knew how persuasive and persistent Chloe could be when she needed to be…when it was necessary to fulfill her wants. She must have finally worn down the poor owner with her sad tale of her grandmother and no one else having a vacancy, Jack figured. He had seen her in action on many occasions in Southampton when this part of Chloe's personality came out…Anne Cartwright had never stood a chance, Jack thought, as he chuckled to himself.

As he read on into the last few paragraphs, Jack saw a photo that Woser had closed the piece with, which told of Harold Grant, the man who had been the first alleged victim of room 33 back in 1925, shortly after The Excelsior opened its doors to the upper crust of Britain. Little was known of Grant, then or now, Woser sighted. All he really emphasized was that the few hours Grant had spent in room 33 set a historical precedent for all future residents of the room. He winced when he thought of it, but what came to Jack was that old commercial for the roach poison that had made its way to England from The States:

"The roach motel. Roaches check in, but they don't check out!"

The photo was an unremarkable shot of Harold Grant from better times, long before he had made the unfortunate decision to stay at The Excelsior. He was looking serious in the shot, and all that Jack could think of was how average and ordinary the man looked. The kind of man, that if you passed him on the street, you would have hardly even remembered anything about him. Grant was forgettable, Jack supposed, but in the background of the photo he spied something quite the opposite. The article had been reproduced from its original source, obviously, but as Jack looked with great focus, what he saw was not due to the reproduction of the copy. Just off Grant's left shoulder and forming a cloud-like mist behind him, was a disturbing black shadow. Despite the warmth of his little flat, Jack found himself racked with a chill that had settled tightly onto the base of his neck.

How Did You Miss This, Woser, You Hack?

Jack massaged his neck and the icy mass broke up and trickled away. The overwhelming sensation of fear and alarm, however did not. Jack was not prone to being easily spooked, but he suddenly had the sick feeling that something about the tales of room 33 might actually have some validity after all. Without realizing it, Jack saw that he had tucked his hands under his armpits to warm his finger as they trembled. And it was not just his hands. Jack stood quickly to pace about as his whole body seemed to be shaking as he tried to figure out what it was in that photo he had spotted that had just freaked him big time. In the bigger picture, he knew it was that amorphous, cottony-looking shadow that seemed to hang over Harold Grant. *But what the hell was the thing?*

Maybe he had just imagined it…it was an old photo, after all. Probably just some photocopy artifact Jack thought as he moved to the sofa near Mortimer. The cat moved to his lap, and Jack exhaled deeply to shake off the anxiety that was threatening to take over. When a teenager, Jack had suffered some mild anxiety attacks. They were attributed partly to normal adolescence and partly to his fear of abandonment as he began to truly face his adoptive status on a deeper emotional level. A therapist had eased him through those black days, and until today, Jack was sure they had vanished forever.

The waves of dread and panic that were flowing through his body now, though, were making Jack yearn for the mild episodes he had had as an adolescent. As he stroked Mortimer, he stared back across the room at the open laptop. He could not actually see the photo that he had left visible on the screen, but there was a magnetic force of some ilk coupled with a voice only Jack could hear, calling him back. His rational mind was now in an all too real battle with his irrational subconscious as Jack looked for a cease fire between the two. He shuddered slightly as he labored to catch his breath and wait for his pulse to slow.

He set Mortimer gently aside and rose to go back. His legs quavered just a hair as he moved with a combination of resolve and hesitation back to the desk. Using the desk and the back of the chair to steady his awkward gait, Jack eased into the chair and closed his eyes, praying with all his might that all the reading he had just done together with Chloe's phone call had been responsible for some sort of visual hallucination. The problem was Jack was not much of a believer in God, nor did he think for even a second that what he had seen just minutes ago was a hallucination.

He lay his sweaty palms face-down on the table on either side of the laptop and took a deep breath as he cautiously opened his eyes again to look at the photo. It was not overly shocking when the photo had not changed, but Jack still felt this hard ball of terror knot up in his stomach, threatening to dislodge his morning coffee. Right there it was. The mild-mannered Harold Grant, looking calmly and patiently into the camera, perhaps posing for some portrait or other purpose. And right behind him, a looming shadow. It had no real form or definition and if he had not known it firmly in his gut as being otherwise, Jack might have convinced himself it was a lighting effect from the photographer.

But deep down he knew it was no lighting aberration. He looked again, now that the bulk of his shock was over. He turned the screen this way and that, but the apparition behind Harold Grant never wavered. *How in the hell had Woser, or anyone else for that matter failed to see this?* Jack was finding his unflappable denial of the paranormal cracking at its foundation. Based on everything, how could this not be the only possible explanation? What was it that Conan Doyle had made a signature quote in his Sherlock Holmes series…

"When you have eliminated the impossible, whatever remains, however improbable, must be the truth…"

Jack felt truly ill as the well-worn line from countless film remakes of the classic books echoed through his mind. But what absolutely terrified and was threatening to paralyze him into inaction was that he was sure that Chloe was in serious trouble in The Excelsior. He could not explain how he knew this, but he did nevertheless. Jack rose from his seat, not bothering to shut off his computer. He snatched up his cell phone and called Chloe, but the call would not go through. Several more attempts gave Jack the same result and he cursed the technology.

He paged through his call log and found the number Chloe had given him for The Excelsior. However, when he dialed it up he just got a recording that the number had either been disconnected or was out of service. Jack got the number for the hotel from directory assistance and tried that, figuring Chloe had messed up with the one she had given him. The call went through, but all he got was this annoying recording. He realized it was Christmas Day and most likely the staff was just available only for emergencies until tomorrow.

He had to get through to Chloe and warn her if it was not already too late. With no other options that he could think of, Jack threw on his winter coat and grabbed his car keys. He called his boss and said he had come down with the flu overnight. He could tell, even over the phone line, that the man was not buying it, but Jack, at the moment could not have cared less about his job. He hoped he could talk his way back into his boss's good graces later. But for now, he was frantic for Chloe's safety. He dumped some dry food into a dish and set it next to a small bowl of cream for Mortimer as he rushed out of the flat having no idea what he might be walking into or how long he might be away. At this point, even the outlandish idea that he might never return slipped into Jack's brain where it took root and festered.

The day stayed cold and overcast as Jack pushed his little car to the limit as he raced north to Blackpool. Fortunately, all normal people were snugged safely away in their homes as they opened presents and gorged themselves on holiday feasts, so Jack had little if any traffic to slow him on his trip. As he neared Birmingham and approached Stoke-On-Trent, the overcast day began to shower Jack with flurries, and by the time he had reached the outskirts of Chorley, the flurries had morphed into a full-blown winter storm. Jack fought to keep his lightweight car on the road as strong winds buffeted him first one way and then the other as the snow blew horizontally, making visibility almost nil.

The wind eased slightly as he arrived in Blackpool, but the snow continued to fall. Jack was totally unfamiliar with the streets in Blackpool, but it was a small place and his GPS led him to The Excelsior perfectly. The rear wheels of his car slid dangerously to one side as he drove too quickly over a patch of icy slush, but Jack regained control of the car just before he spun beyond recovery. He felt his heart leap at the near mishap and slowed as he drove down Lytham Road toward his destination. The hotel loomed ominously before Jack as he shut off the car and got out. He squinted hard against the blowing snow as he slammed the door and ran to the entrance. He had expected his next hurdle to be gaining access to the hotel on Christmas Day, when the staff was seemingly just on call.

However, when Jack grasped the handle of the front door, he nearly fell backward as the door opened easily. He rushed through the opening into the warm interior and threw back the hood on his coat. The lobby was empty and the front desk was unoccupied as well. It seemed inconceivable to Jack that they had left the building open, and on top of that apparently unattended. Perhaps whoever was manning the reception desk was just checking on a guest or doing some other routine task. At this point, Jack hardly cared. Actually, it made his task much easier not having to explain his unfounded intuition that his girlfriend, who they had put up in the cursed room 33, might be in mortal danger from a demonic presence that had been around for almost a hundred years.

Getting locked up for being insane was just not on Jack's schedule for the day. He blasted past the check-in desk and entered the hallway just off to the side. He had no idea where room 33 was exactly, but there was just the single hallway and it seemed likely that the room was located on the ground floor. As Jack was about halfway down the corridor, the noxious odor of sulfur hit him like a wall. He felt his stomach heave, but he gritted his teeth and forced the rising gorge from his stomach back down as he covered his mouth and nose with his arm. The rooms ran in a predictable numerical order and Jack could see that the door to what had to be room 33 was ajar.

The closer he got, the worse the stench got, but he managed to cry out for Chloe regardless. With no response, Jack had a sinking feeling of what he would find inside, and he nearly faltered, sure he was way too late to save her. From somewhere, though, Jack summoned his inner reserves and rushed into the room as the door banged open and bounced off the wall. Jack stopped as if he had run into an invisible barrier and just sank to his knees near the bed. On the mattress, splayed across its width was Chloe. The look on her face was like nothing Jack had ever seen before and he hoped never to have to see anywhere again.

Her facial features were twisted into a horrible grimace of pain, panic, desperation, horror, and fear. The covers on the bed were balled into a knot, where her feet had become entangled as if she might have been trying to escape from whatever it was that had ended her life and caused her last moments on earth to be indescribably horrendous and dreadful. Jack shook his head back and forth, trying to deny what he was looking at before he leaned back and let out the most piercing and blood-curdling scream imaginable. He slid forward and put his hands on Chloe's cold, clammy exposed leg as he cried harder than he could ever recall. His vision was blurry from his tears, but as Jack looked up above the bed, he saw the black shadow...the last thing Jack recalled before he passed out.

Early Bird Notification List

Thank you for reading The Haunting of Excelsior Hotel. To join my early bird notification list of all my new releases, please click on the links below:

http://www.rileyamitrani.com

Please like my Facebook fan page:

https://www.facebook.com/RileyAmitraniOfficial/

Please follow me on Twitter:

https://www.twitter.com/RileyAmitrani/

Please follow me on Amazon Author Central:

http://amazon.com/author/rileyamitrani

Books By Riley Amitrani

The Haunting of Prescott House

Click the links below to download on Amazon:

Amazon.com

Amazon.co.uk

The Haunting of Luciano House

Click the links below to download on Amazon:

Amazon.com

Amazon.co.uk

The Haunting of Perry Property

Click the links below to download on
Amazon:

Amazon.com

Amazon.co.uk

The Haunting of Alfred House

Click the links below to download on
Amazon:

Amazon.com

Amazon.co.uk

The Haunting of Woodchester Mansion

Click the links below to download on
Amazon:

Amazon.com

Amazon.co.uk

Haunted House Horror: 4 Book Haunted House Box Set

Click the links below to download on Amazon:

Amazon.com

Amazon.co.uk

Haunted Halloween Collection 16 Book Box Set

Click the links below to download on Amazon:

Amazon.com

Amazon.co.uk

The Haunting of Magnolia House

Click the links below to download on Amazon:

Amazon.com

Amazon.co.uk

The Haunting of Excelsior Hotel

Click the links below to download on Amazon:

Amazon.com

Amazon.co.uk

The Haunting of Prescott House Preview

Prologue

5th September 1959

Prescott House, near Bristol,

England

7:34 PM

Martin Prescott threw his neck back to pour the last of his whisky down his throat. He slammed the glass down on his desk, not caring when it shattered from the force. Underneath the shards of glass was a pile of unopened letters. He was in his study, shut away from the rest of the house where his wife and two children went about their evening oblivious to Martin's pain. He got up and headed to his drinks cabinet. It was once filled with a most impressive spirit collection. Now it was a hoard of near-empty bottles. He picked up a bottle of whisky and shook the last dregs into a fresh glass, took a packet of Camels out of his pocket and lit one.

"Daddy?" A voice called at the door. Martin spun around to see his youngest girl, Elizabeth, watching him from the hallway. In her tiny hand, she clutched a picture she had drawn for him.

"Go back to your room, Libby." Martin turned from her, not wanting her to see him in this state. Libby pouted, at four years old she did not care to see her father unhappy, nor could she begin to understand the reason why. She dropped the piece of paper she was carrying on the floor and toddled out of the room.

Martin went to the door and slammed it shut behind him. He picked up the drawing. It was difficult to decipher the scribblings of a four-year-old, but he could make out her intention. She had drawn herself and her sibling, Rose playing outside in the garden. She had scrawled red to depict the rose bushes which gave their house a sense of traditional English grandeur. Inside the yellow house she had drawn a figure who must be Sally, Martin's wife. She was standing in the doorway, keeping a careful eye on her girls, in the picture as she does in life. But where was Martin? Libby had drawn him alone in his study. Martin screwed the picture up and threw it at the paper basket. Taking a last drag of his cigarette before he stubbed it out, he straightened his tie then headed down to the dining room where he found his wife.

"So you're joining me for dinner then?" Sally said, arching a perfectly pencilled brow. She poured a glass of wine for herself and for him. Martin noticed that the bottle was almost empty. The roast dinner on the table had long gone cold. Martin sat down without a word and started to eat, not bothering to put his napkin on his lap. The dining room was as opulent as the rest of the house. The dark oak furniture was antique and above them hung a glass chandelier which shone warm light around the room. But the atmosphere was cold, with only the sound of the grandfather clock ticking to fill the silence, until Sally spoke.

"I need to go into town tomorrow to get a new dress." Sally said. "I've been invited for tea with Sandra and Louise and can't wear something they have seen before." Martin carried on eating. "So I really need some money. I'm sick of darning my old dresses and pretending that they're not the same ones my friends have seen before. Are you listening to me?" She raised her voice.

"You have a whole wardrobe full of dresses." Martin said. "You don't need another."

"I don't need another? I'm your wife, not a servant who should have to ask every time I need something. You should be providing for me."

"I have to pay off this ludicrous house you had us buy. You wanted this, didn't you?" He got up, knocking his chair over as he did, and stood above Sally. "Didn't you?" His voice roared and echoed through the house.

"I want a husband and a father. A real man." Sally stood up. Martin raised his hand and slapped her, the force of which made her fall back into her seat. "You said you would never do that again." Sally said, clutching her red cheek. "Tomorrow I'm taking the children to my mother's." Sally ran out of the room.

Martin was enraged. He headed back to his study, where he picked up a bottle of liquor. He swigged it straight from the bottle. Something caught his eye out the window. He turned the light off and looked outside.

There was a shadow of a man outside on the street. He was standing next to a tree, smoking and watching the house. No doubt he was one of the men Martin owed money to for unpaid gambling debts. He had done this all to keep his bitch of a wife happy. The wife who had threatened to leave him just because he couldn't afford to keep up with her spending habits. His head was spinning, his eyes blurred but he knew what to do. He took a final gulp of liquor. He headed over to the drinks table, on which was a box of cigars. He turned the box upside down causing the few remaining expensive cigars to fall on the floor. A silver key also fell out. He took the key and used it to unlock the bottom draw of his desk. He removed an item from it, concealed in a black bag.

He headed upstairs, past the staircase to his children's bedroom where his pretty blonde daughters slept peacefully, oblivious to their parents' problems. He got to the opulent room he shared with his wife. The four-poster bed was still made. She hadn't gone to bed yet. He noticed light coming out under the door to the bathroom. He tried the handle. It was locked. He kicked the door. He heard Sally scream inside. He kicked it again and again. On the third try it sprung open revealing Sally in the bath. With her blonde curls loose around her and eyes wide, she looked vulnerable.

"What are you doing? Are you insane?" Sally said, shrinking back in the bath. Martin did not respond. He pulled a silver handgun out of the bag. He held it up and aimed it at Sally's head. "No, please," Sally begged. He shot, the silencer dulling the sound of the bullet. It flew out and landed in Sally's skull, causing bone and brain matter to splatter across the white tiles. She sank lifeless into the water as it slowly became a bath of blood.

"Daddy?" Elizabeth stood in the doorway, she was dressed in her pyjamas, her doll in hand. "What's happened to Mummy?"

"Close your eyes, Libby." Martin said as he raised the gun a second time.

Prescott Mansion

30th April 2016
Cambridge
Cambridgeshire
England
3:10 PM

"Come on! What is taking so long?" Amanda reached into the car's open window and pressed the hooter. It was a new model Mini Cooper in red that she had recently received as gift from her father. She leaned against it, cigarette in hand and sunglasses on. It was parked outside the student digs which her friends Kim and Gemma shared, situated on a cobbled side street a stone's throw from the River Cam. As she waited, a group of Chinese tourists came down the street. They paused to take photos of Amanda. She had long blonde hair and was dressed in cut-off denim shorts with a shirt tied up to expose her midriff. Leaning against her car and outside a quintessentially British town house, she looked like a model awaiting a shoot. But instead of basking in their attention she repaid their curiosity by giving them the finger.

"Amanda! Do you really need to swear

at the tourists?" Kim said as she came out of the house. She was dressed in a suit jacket, blouse and chinos. She carried a large hold-all over her shoulder. "And are those shoes really suitable for a drive?" Amanda looked down at her chunky wedges and rolled her eyes. Kim was too sensible for her own good.

"Where's Gemma?" Amanda asked.

"I'm ready." Gemma said as she stepped out of the house. She wheeled a small suitcase behind her with one hand and was carrying a precariously balanced pile of Law books in the other.

"Jesus Gemma, are you heading off to court? This is supposed to be a holiday." Amanda grabbed some of the books from her, and tossed them in the boot.

"No. This isn't a holiday; we're going away to study remember?" Kim said.

"Exams are only three weeks away and some of us actually want to pass."

"I'm sorry, Amanda, I just want to be as prepared as possible." Gemma took a piece of paper and a pen out of her pocket. "I just need to double check that I have all the recommended reading materials, spare memory sticks, flash cards-"

"I'm sure you have." Amanda interrupted, grabbing her suitcase and putting it in the boot. "Let's get out on the road. I'm sick of this city."

"Gemma just wants to be prepared, Amanda. I doubt you've thought about what supplies we need to last us." Kim said, glaring at Amanda. Kim and Amanda, being the highest grading law students in their year at Cambridge University, had an unspoken rivalry. Kim, daughter of a top family of Solicitors from London had the law in her blood. She aced every exam and won every possible scholarship. Amanda on the other hand was the daughter of a model and a wealthy TV producer. She had inherited her mother's looks and the favour of her father's friends. Amanda did well in life, being well connected, and Kim resented her for it. It was only their mutual friendship with Gemma that kept them from fighting.

"As it happens, I have come prepared." Amanda shot Kim her professionally whitened smile as she pulled a blanket off a crate in the boot. In it were crates of beer and wine. "Let's go."

"Are you sure this is the right way?" Gemma said. It did appear that the unmarked gravel road Amanda had taken them down couldn't possibly lead to their destination. Amanda leaned forward, struggling to see through the heavy rain shower relentlessly hitting her windscreen. It was after ten and the sun had long set.

"This is where the Sat Nav is taking me." Amanda said, starting to regret this whole idea. Amanda's father, who orchestrated all Amanda's achievements, had become worried that Amanda's shortcomings may finally be showing. He had paid for everything; the all-girls private school and college, the best tutors, and arranged internships. It was all to give his daughter, who lacked any real drive and ambition, the best start in life. But what he couldn't help her with was passing her final exams at Cambridge University. That she had to do for herself. What he had done was arrange for her and her friends to get out of Cambridge for a few weeks. A friend of his had agreed to let his daughter and her friends rent a house he owned. Amanda had been reluctant to take him up on the offer at first, but being promised free rein of a large house in the city of Bath had appealed to her. But why was the Sat Nav taking her past Bath and towards a forest just outside of Bristol?

"I thought you said we would be in the Royal Crescent?" Kim said. She smiled at the prospect of Amanda being taken down a few notches. "Did Daddy not want to pay up?" Kim looked to the back of the car where Gemma sat. Gemma, however had her nose in a book and headphones on, oblivious to the catty conversation taking place at the front of the car.

"Well, I'm sure wherever he has booked us will be grand. Father has impeccable taste." Amanda said. She had assumed they would be staying in a Georgian townhouse and would be able to spend their days shopping and going out for brunch instead of studying. Inwardly she was panicked at the thought of where they were driving. She hated forests and the outdoors and doubted she would find a house befitting of her status in this one. In fact, they hadn't even passed a house for the last two miles.

The Sat Nav beeped, informing them that they had reached their destination. Amanda looked through the rain and could make out a shape ahead. They were approaching a dilapidated mansion, which once would have been a fine art deco house. The red brick work was covered in vines; The roof was covered in moss; The windows were dirty and the paintwork was peeling off the frames. Rose bushes in the garden had grown into thick gnarled branches with brown-spotted diseased red petals. Amanda pulled up on the weed covered driveway, the car jolting as it went over the broken bricks underneath.

"Wow. Where the hell have you bought us, Amanda? This place looks abandoned." Kim got her phone out and took a photo, no doubt to send to her friends back in the city, who would laugh at Amanda's embarrassment. "This isn't exactly the five-star accommodation we were promised."

"I don't understand. Father promised me we would be staying in luxury accommodation." Amanda said, checking that the destination was correct.

"Can we just get inside? It's been a long journey." Gemma said, setting her book down.

"Oh no I am not setting foot in this house. There must be some mistake." Amanda got her phone ready to give her father a piece of her mind until he agreed to let them stay at the nearest five-star spa instead. When she looked at her phone however, her father had sent her a message, predicting her discontent at his choice of accommodation.

Amanda, I know this isn't what you were expecting, but it is what you need. This house will give you the isolation you need to do your revision. I can only do so much to help you in life. Now you must use your brain and initiative. Oh, and don't even think about leaving before the end of the three weeks, I have blocked your credit cards. You will stay and you will study.

Amanda's face reddened when she read the message. She gripped the phone tightly in her hands till her knuckles turned white. She then composed herself and turned to Kim and Gemma.

"I've changed my mind." Amanda said, flashing a smile. "I fancy an adventure." Amanda got out of the car, ignoring the relentless rain. Kim and Gemma followed. As the lights of the car turned off, they were plunged into darkness.

"You didn't bring a torch by any chance?" Kim asked Gemma.

"No, I didn't think it would be needed." Gemma replied, a faceless voice in the dark. Gemma gripped Kim's hand in the dark, and they followed in the direction that they hoped was the house. They felt their way across the uneven path with careful footsteps. Kim could sense Amanda was just ahead of them.

"Amanda, have you found the door yet?" Kim asked.

"Yes it's here." Amanda replied. Kim reached out and begrudgingly found Amanda's hand. The safety of traveling in numbers trumping their rivalry.

"Well, can you let us in?" Kim said. A bolt of lightning illuminated them for a moment. Amanda stood drenched through, mascara running down her face. They were standing under the porch of the house, a grand wooden door in front of them. Lightning struck again. A metal sign hung next to the door, Amanda wiped the dirt from it with her sleeve. It said "Prescott House." Before she could take anything else in, they were plunged back into darkness.

"I have a slight problem. I don't have a key." Amanda said.

"Haha, very funny. Just let us in." Kim said, not in the mood for games from the ever-manipulative Amanda.

"I'm not being funny. Father didn't send me a key."

"Then how did you think we were going to get in the house? Was Lurch going to meet us at the door?" Kim was used to Amanda's reliance in the world revolving around her, but this foresight was unquestionably stupid.

"I'm getting cold now. Can I go back and wait in the car?" Gemma said. Kim realised that Gemma's hand had become deathly cold.

"No!" Amanda shouted. "If Father didn't give me a key, it must have been for good reason." She tried the door but it was locked. "It must be hidden out here somewhere." Amanda felt on the wet floor for a door mat for it to be hidden under, or a plant pot under which it might be concealed. She frantically pawed at the floor.

"This is ridiculous." Kim said. Kim was about to turn to leave, when another lightning bolt struck, illuminating the sky once again. Kim and Gemma saw Amanda on hands and knees on the floor, her clothes muddy. Over her stood a man dressed in a black cloak that was draped over his head, his face in shadow. He towered over Amanda, his arms raised. In his hand he held a weapon ready to strike.

The story continues…

Amazon.com

Amazon.co.uk

The Haunting of Magnolia House Preview

Prologue

3rd August 1972

Magnolia House

London

6:54 PM

    Evelyn Summers stood in her silk underwear in front of her bedroom mirror. She held up a floor length mustard dress in front of her and looked at her reflection. She threw it on the bed then held up a pink chiffon dress and did the same. Neither were quite right. She wished she had bought herself something new to wear. Evelyn and her husband were hosting a dinner party that night. She had prepared the prawn cocktails, and the duck a l'orange was in the oven. She was ready to serve snowball cocktails and brandy, and the table had been set. The last step was deciding on what to wear.

    Evelyn heard the sound of a car

approaching. She went over to the window and drew back the net curtain. She looked out onto the street, and the empty parking space below her house. The car was the next-door neighbour arriving home in his Ford Cortina. She breathed out a sigh of relief at having some time left. Evelyn watched him get out of his car and go to the front door to be greeted by his wife. Evelyn and her husband lived in the end house on a very nice street where each newly built house looked the same as the next. They had only recently moved in, and were keen to impress their new neighbours that night. Evelyn wandered over to her dressing table and picked up her bottle of Charlie fragrance. As she was spraying it on her neck, she saw a face in the mirror. She was being watched.

"Mummy?" Evelyn turned at the voice. Her four-year-old daughter, Sarah, was stood in the doorway watching her. In her hand was her favourite doll Rebecca. She was carrying her by her patchy hair. The doll's face was painted with rosy cheeks and lips curved into a grotesque smile. Its blue glass eyes were looking in different directions. Evelyn hated that doll. In Sarah's other hand was a ball. "Mummy, I want to play." She threw the ball towards her mum. It hit the floor and slowly rolled towards her. Evelyn bent down to pick up the ball and held it out for Sarah. She noticed Sarah had a wet trail coming from her nose.

"No darling, Mummy is getting ready to go out. Go downstairs and play." Evelyn stood up, keen to not get her silk underwear dirty. She picked up the ball and threw it out of the room and down the hallway. She turned her back on Sarah, who walked away. Evelyn turned back to the mirror. She decided on the mustard dress and slipped it on. She sat at her dressing table and started to apply her make up. Downstairs she could hear Sarah singing baa baa black sheep. Evelyn got up and put on a record. Diana Ross always helped to get her in the mood to go out. She selected a peach lipstick and carefully applied it. She then styled her hair, and selected some shoes to wear. She was ready. She turned off her record. It was quiet downstairs.

"Are you alright Sarah?" She called. There was no answer. Evelyn went to the hallway and called down again. There was no response. She went downstairs and into the kitchen. The hatch to their cellar was open. Evelyn approached the cellar and looked down the stairs. It was dark, the light to the cellar not working. She took a couple of steps down and her eyes started to adjust to the light. She looked at the bottom of the staircase. She could see Sarah's doll, Rebecca lying on the floor, her face still in that unnatural smirk.

Magnolia House

20th May 2017
Magnolia House
London
4:42 PM

"Be careful with that one, it has fragile on it for a reason," Jess said to the delivery man in reaction to hearing the sound of glass jangling from the rain sodden cardboard box he was carrying. She turned to her partner Mickey and rolled her eyes. But Mickey hadn't seen, he was too busy staring at his phone.

"So Jess, how does it feel to be a homeowner?" Mickey approached, shoving his phone camera towards her. "Come on, I want to make a vlog about today." Jess rolled her eyes and pushed the camera away.

"Maybe later then? Hey, at least I've found this box," Mikey said, as he pointed at a box labelled 'kettle'. He went inside the house, camera in one hand and the box in the other. Mickey was excited. Ever since they had met two years ago, Jess had known Mickey's dream was to buy an old house to renovate. He would have loved to have bought a former Victorian orphanage or a converted church, but this 1970's terraced house would have to do. He had decided to make a video log of the moving in and renovation process. Jess watched him tilting his phone around, looking at every wall and ceiling, whilst talking to the camera.

Sarah tilted her umbrella back and looked at their new home. The name 'Magnolia House' was ironic for a house which was surrounded by weeds and gnarled branches. The crazy paving of the driveway was uneven and damaged, with weeds sprouting up within the cracks. It led to an integral garage with an avocado green painted door which was covered in years of dirt. The two-storey high 1970's house situated on a street of near identical terraced houses. Their most prominent feature was their angular sloped roofs which looked like a row of shark fins. The house had plastic white cladding which was covered in green grime. The white painted front door was peeling, revealing the bare wood underneath. At clouded windows hung yellowed net curtains. In the grey February rain the house looked even less appealing. But Mickey had fallen in love with it. It had been empty since the seventies and nothing had been changed inside. Jess was just pleased they had got a good deal on it. As Jess was looking, she noticed the net at next doors window twitching. She was being watched. She raised her hand and gave a friendly wave. The curtain stopped moving.

"Where do you want this one?" One of the removal men broke her thoughts. They were carrying her antique desk, her most treasured possession and the only piece of furniture they owned which hadn't been a flat pack.

"Upstairs in the second bedroom," she said, following them in and watching tentatively in case they damaged it.

Jess had forgotten just how much work the house needed. The walls were covered in textured wallpaper that felt like sandpaper when you touched it. The light bulb in the hallway was covered in a lampshade with more tassels then a cabaret show, and the carpet was a pattern that could bring on a hallucination. The air smelt damp like an old church. The living room was wallpapered in a circular orange and yellow pattern. There was a gas fire on one wall. Although there was no furniture in the house, there were still paintings on the walls and a trio of wooden ducks on the wall, as if in flight. There was a large mirror above the fireplace that had a large crack in one corner and rust around the edges.

"Hey, nothing that we can't change. This place will feel like our own soon enough," Mickey said guessing her thoughts. He slipped an arm around her waist and passed her a mug of coffee. He could always sense what she was feeling. Jess turned to him and smiled.

"You're right. We can make this our home," Jess said. She realised the removal men were hovering in the hallway waiting. Jess went and paid them.

"Shall we bring Bella in?" Mickey said. Bella was their tortoiseshell house cat, and Jess's baby. Mickey went to get her cat carrier from the car. The stress of moving had caused her to cry for the whole journey. Jess went into the kitchen and checked they had everything ready. It was the first time since moving she had been into the kitchen. It was bright with double doors to the garden. The units were avocado in colour. On the floor was a large red rug which looked as out of place as it was unhygienic. Her litter tray was near the back door, the basket was in the living room and so was her cat climbing frame. Jess ignored all of these dated remains and looked at the cat climbing frame. Jess was pleased that her Bella would have more room to roam. That was about the only positive she could think of about the house. The front door shut with a bang.

"It's ok Bella, you crazy mog. Calm down." It was Mickey brining Bella inside. He was carrying her in her cat carrier which was covered with a blanket. Inside she wailed and scratched. "I think you need to take her." He passed the carrier to Jess.

"Hey Bella, are you ok?" Jess set her carrier down on the sofa and knelt next to her. She lifted up the blanket and looked inside. Bella was stood up, back arched and hair on end. "Maybe I should leave her in here a bit longer until she calms down?" Jess took the blanket off but left the carrier shut. Mickey had walked off, his patience with Bella growing thin. He was stood at the back door. "Are you ok?" Jess said.

"I'm just working out what all these keys are for," Mickey said. Jess looked at the large keyring full of keys that the estate agent had given them. Mickey identified the one which opened the back door. It creaked open. The rain had subsided, the ground left covered in muddy puddles. Outside the small patio was covered in weeds. There were a few discarded plastic plant pots in the corner. Behind the garden they could see the London skyline in the distance. Jess went and joined Mickey and looked past the garden to the grey tower blocks and tall cranes in the distance. It comforted her and made her feel lonely all at once. As ugly as their house was, it was a sensible purchase. A run-down house in the suburbs which one day would be worth a lot more. As they looked she heard a noise next door. It was someone in the garden. Jess raised her finger to her lips to signify Mickey to not talk. She crept over to the wooden fence and looked through a small hole into next doors garden. This garden was full of plants and flowers. In fact, they had taken over the small garden making it a forest. She looked through the foliage and could make out a petite, hunched over woman with patchy grey hair. She was wearing a moth-eaten cardigan. She was bent over, shears in hand. As Jess watched the woman stood up and turned around, looking at the fence exactly where Jess was peeking through. Jess jumped back. She knew that the hole was too small for the woman to see through, but that didn't stop her feeling tense.

"Let's go back inside," Jess said. They went back into the kitchen and Jess went into the adjoining living room. She peeked into the cat carrier, Bella was now still. Mickey was busying himself in the kitchen, so Jess decided to go and explore upstairs. She went up the staircase, which creaked with every step, and into the main bedroom. Their bed was in the middle, surrounded by boxes arranged haphazardly by the removal men. She inspected the brown floral wallpaper that was peeling from the corners. The air was thick with dust. Jess went over to the window and pulled back the dirty net. She opened the window as wide as it would go. Fresh post rain air gushed into the room. She looked out across the street. Staring back was a row of identical houses. The street below was full of parked people carriers. An old man walked past pushing a trolley that creaked with each slow shuffle he took. They were in suburbia. Jess sighed. She already missed their old flat. It was a small one bedroom flat in Camden which had cost them a small fortune to rent. But she loved the hustle of being in the middle of everything and two minutes away from the tube. The smell of street food cooking, the sound of the market traders, and how the flat shook sometimes when a train went past. But they couldn't afford to buy anywhere in Camden, it was only by moving further afield that they could afford it. And this area was supposed to be up and coming. Whatever that meant.

Jess stepped away from the window and went to the second bedroom. This room was covered in ugly wooden cladding. Up against the wall was her desk. She ran her hands over the aged wood. Jess was a writer and this desk was where she had always worked. As she was looking around she heard a noise above her head. She looked up at the ceiling. It was a creaking sound coming from the attic. Jess reached up on tip toes and touched the ceiling. She thought she could sense something move up there.

"Jess?" Mickey called her. "Come here." She turned around and headed to the door.

"Yes Mickey?" She called down.

"Come and let the cat out so we can put the dinner on," he called. Mickey wasn't asking out of concern for her, he was only thinking of his own stomach. Bella was always fed first so she didn't try to eat their food when they were eating. Jess glanced up at the celling then headed downstairs and into the living room. She looked in the cat carrier. Bella was asleep. She opened the door and put an arm in, scooping the sleeping Bella up into her arms. She was a warm mass of fuzz, and Jess felt instantly relaxed holding her.

"Come on, let's get you some food," Jess said as she carried her into the kitchen. Mickey was chopping vegetables and adding them into a pot. It smelt like bolognaise. Jess shut the door behind her to keep the smell out. He had laid her bowl of food and water out on the floor ready for Bella. She scratched Bella behind her ear until she started to stir. "Come on girl, time to wake up," Jess said. Bella woke and dug her claws hard into Jess's arm. Jess yelped and dropped Bella onto the floor. Bella ran around the small kitchen in circles.

"Pick that bloody cat up!" Mickey

shouted.

"I'm trying," Jess shouted back. She opened the door to the living room to retrieve Bella's carrier, then headed back into the kitchen. Bella was standing in a corner, back arched, hair on end and hissing. Jess crept closer and closer with the box.

"Here give it to me," Mickey snatched it out of her hand. "You distract her."

"Come on Bella, calm down," Jess said as she held her hand under her chin at her. Bella hissed at her and tried to swipe her hand. Jess jumped to one side and tripped over the ghastly rug, causing it to slip out from underneath her feet.

"I've got her, stupid cat," Mickey said as he shut the cat carrier on her. "You're going back in the living room to calm down. Are you ok?" He said to Jess, finally noticing her on the floor, where she had fallen.

"Yeah, I'm ok," Jess said, sitting up. She looked at her elbow, it was sore from knocking it on the floor. Her hand also hurt from where Bella had scratched her. It was not like Bella to be so aggressive, but then again, she had never moved house. "That's it, I want to get rid of this stupid rug now," Jess said. It was easier to blame the rug than to discuss Bella's aggression. "Who would put a rug in a kitchen anyway? It's most unsanitary. I don't care if the floor is bare underneath."

Jess started to roll up the rug, causing a cloud of dust to rise up over the room. She coughed as she worked. Mickey helped her roll it up. They then opened the back door and put it in the back garden.

"I think I had better sweep this up before dinner," Jess said. She got a brush and dustpan out and started to sweep the floor. It wasn't concrete like she had expected from a relatively modern house, it was wooden. She was pleased, this meant they might be able to polish up the floor rather than lay a whole new one. As she swept she noticed a gap in the floor, she followed it along, it was a straight line that went into a right angle. She followed it around and saw it made a square. Then she found a metal handle in the middle.

"You won't believe this," Jess said to Mickey who was cooking dinner with his back turned to her. "-But I think I've found a door or a cupboard or… something." Mickey turned to look. He took out his phone, held it up and filmed Jess as she examined the floor. It was a door of about two feet wide each way. Jess lifted up the handle and pulled it. It was locked.

"What do you think it is?" Jess said.

"It must be a cellar, of some kind of underground storage at the very least. I can't believe this wasn't picked up by the surveyors, what on earth did we pay them for?" Mickey said. "Here, let me try." He grabbed hold of the handle and tried to pull it up, but to no avail.

"But this is good, isn't it?" Jess said. "Whatever it is could add value to the home?"

"That set of keys, have you got them?" Mickey said. Jess handed them to him. He tried each one in turn. "It's no good, there isn't one which fits." Jess was secretly glad. She looked down at the trap door. She really didn't like the idea that there could be a secret room beneath their feet.

The story continues…

Amazon.com

Amazon.co.uk

Copyright Notice

The Haunting of Excelsior Hotel

By

Riley Amitrani

http://www.rileyamitrani.com

http://www.beyondoriginal.com

PUBLISHED BY:

Beyond Original LLC and Riley Amitrani

from the copyright owner and publisher of this book.

This is a work of fiction. All characters, names, places and events are the product of the author's imagination or used fictitiously.

———————————————————

—————

Printed in Great Britain
by Amazon

41352406R00090